For Rosie
who lent me her babies,
Lucy and Nicola
M.W.

For Ruth
and Rowan,
my real inspiration
P.D.

First published 1990 by Walker Books Ltd
87 Vauxhall Walk, London SE11 5HJ

This edition published 2001

4 6 8 10 9 7 5 3

Text © 1990 Martin Waddell
Illustrations © 1990 Penny Dale

Printed in Singapore

British Library Cataloguing in Publication Data:
a catalogue record for this book
is available from the British Library

ISBN 0-7445-8163-X

Rosie's Babies

written by
Martin Waddell

illustrated by
Penny Dale

WALKER BOOKS
AND SUBSIDIARIES
LONDON · BOSTON · SYDNEY

Mum was putting the baby to bed and Rosie said, "I've got two babies and you've only got one." "Two, including you," said Mum. "I'm not a baby, I'm four years old," said Rosie. "Tell me about your babies," Mum said.

And Rosie said,
"My babies live in a bird's
nest and they are nearly as
big as me. They go out in
the garden all by themselves
and sometimes they make
me cross!"
"Do they?" said Mum.
"Yes. When they do silly things!"
said Rosie.
"What silly things do they do?"
asked Mum.

And Rosie said,
"My babies climbed a big
mountain. That was silly,
because they couldn't get
down. They jumped, and they
bumped on their bottoms!"
"Silly babies," said Mum.
"Did they hurt themselves?"

And Rosie said,
"One of my babies hurt her knee. I bandaged it up and she cried and I said 'Never mind' because I am kind."
"I'm sure you are," said Mum.
"What else do your babies do?"

And Rosie said,
"My babies drive cars that
are real ones and lorries and
dumpers and boats. My babies
are very good drivers."
"What do your babies like
doing best?" asked Mum.

And Rosie said,
"My babies like swings and rockers and dinosaurs. They go to the park when it's dark and there are no mums and dads who can see, only me!"
"Gracious!" said Mum.
"Aren't they scared?"

And Rosie said,
"My babies are scared of the
   big dog, but I'm not.
   I know the big dog. I go
   'Blackie, sit,' and he does."
"They are not very scared then?"
   said Mum.
"My babies know I will look
   after them," said Rosie.
"I'm their mum."
"How do you look after them?"
   Mum asked.

And Rosie said,
"I make their teas and I tell them stories
and I take them for walks and I talk to
them and I tell them that I love them."
"That's a good way to look after babies!"
said Mum. "Do you make them nice
things to eat, like pies?"

And Rosie said,
"My babies make their own pies,
but they never eat them."
"What do they eat?" asked Mum.

And Rosie said,
"My babies eat apples and
apples and apples all the time.
And grapes and pears but they
don't like the pips."
"Most babies don't," said Mum.
"Are you going to tell me
more about your babies?"

And Rosie thought and thought
and thought and then Rosie said,
"My babies have gone to bed."
"Just like this one," said Mum.
"I don't want to talk about my
babies any more because they are
asleep," said Rosie. "I don't want
them to wake up, or they'll cry."
"We could talk very softly,"
said Mum.
"Yes," said Rosie.
"What will we talk about?"
asked Mum.

And Rosie said,
"ME!"